ADVENTURE IN WAYANAD

AUTHOR: KHALIL ISAAC MATHAI

EDITING AND COVER DESIGN: JIBIN JAMES

CHAPTERS......

This page left blank intentionally

1# Train trip to Kozhikode

The girl was tall and stately with an impressive figure. Her long slender limbs and sharp features set her apart from the rest as she queued up for a rail ticket. All men gave her a second glance. A few insolent youths, openly stared.

Her name was Saliba. She had recently graduated in English literature from the Women's College. She would have a month or two to explore options and peek up avenues ahead. Her years in college had been pleasant, to say the least. The BA curriculum had not been overtly challenging. Saliba had played college basket-ball and had captained her team in the final year.

She played well. With her height and grace, she would glide around clumsier opponents scoring baskets with an infuriating ease. There were boisterous crowds of college fans at her every match.   Saliba had a lingering suspicion that half the spectators were there to ogle her shapely, slender, long legs.   She did not care. Saliba was not intimidated by men.

The ticket counter clerk looked at her with insolently intrusive and frank admiration. "Where to?" He asked. "Single to Wayanad", said Saliba. The clerk raised his eyebrows – Wayanad was the latest adventure destination in Kerala Tourism. He tried to strike up a conversation. "I have seen you
play basketball- you play well". He meant to say that she looked great. But in Kerala, such compliments to a girl could create trouble. There was some mumbling down the ticket queue. He quickly passed her the ticket, feasting his eyes on her figure as she walked away to platform.

There was an announcement. The train was drawing up. A motley assorted crowd jostled, milling around the door as some passengers disembarked. A saree clad lady with a tote bag stumbled as she got off the train. She scowled angrily at Saliba who smiled back. There was a rough scramble to embark. Saliba got jostled through the crowd and into the train. Finding a seat was like musical chairs. You needed luck, skill and speed. There were no reservations on short distance trains. You scrambled into one of the 18 coaches in the general compartment. She was lucky to find a window seat for herself. The compartment filled up fast. It was safer to be in a general compartment. Beyond some jostling and hungry stares, you get away unscathed.

She had a four-hour journey ahead. Saliba looked around. With a seat secured, she would be comfortable. It was always nice if you knew someone else in the compartment. There was an additional layer of safety. A couple with their ten-year old son had just boarded the train. All seats were taken. Saliba shifted a bit to make room for the kid near the window. She smiled to herself. She had just got herself a local guardian for the train journey.

The train chugged out of Ernakulum station. The Indian railway network was one of the major contributions of the British. If you were physically fit and not too squeamish, train journeys were convenient, relatively safe and ridiculously cheap. The roads were treacherous. Except for the National Highways, roads tended to be narrow and strategically potholed. Saliba suffered from motion sickness. The exquisite sensitivity of her vestibular system, which offered her divine grace on the basketball court, was a liability in bumpy bus ride. When she travelled by bus, she would pop in an 'Avomine' tab which stabilized her ears but which brought in a mist of drowsiness. Reading during a bus journey was not an option for her. Trains were crowded and the sanitation iffy. Train connectivity however was excellent.

The train slowed to a stop at the next station. Another lot of passengers alighted. Her travelling companion's parents managed to secure two seats for themselves. They reclaimed their progeny. Saliba had the seat to herself. A barrage of vendors selling tea, samosas and other snacks snaked their only way amongst the passengers, aggressively announcing their wares. The boy's parents bought him a Samosa. Saliba was also offered one, but she politely declined. She did not have to watch calories. Her physical exercise regime kept her in shape. The potential bugs she might ingest could trouble her during the coming adventure.

She had with her a magazine sent by her sister-in law. 'The Economist' was possibly the most informative and well written magazine in the world. Issues of the magazine were expensive off the shelf for a college student. Her brother in Australia had offered to send her copies after he read them. The magazine proffered an informed world view, insights into science and the arts, delectable opinion columns and a particularly heart wrenching obituary page. She now proceeded to read it from cover to cover. Saliba loved reading. Her parents had plans to goad her to appear for her civil services examination soon.

Both Saliba's parents were doctors. While she was at school, it was generally assured that she would opt for biology and follow here parent's foot-steps up the Hippocratic aisle. But Saliba had a mind of her own. After her tenth, she opted out of the science stream. While her friends in the mathematics and science groups had struggled between coaching class and school, she had played basketball and read voraciously. Saliba had gone hiking on weekends and had made a trip to Europe. Reading and exploring had proffered her a maturity and fostered in her, a depth of character unusual in today's youth. Saliba sometimes wondered if it were a mistake, forsaking a professional course. The NEET exam had simplified the medical entrance procedure. If you aced the scores, you would walk into one of the country's premier institutes. If your scores were mediocre, parents could pay a capitation fee to slot you into one of the myriad private colleges mushrooming across the country. 4 years of hard work and you would be looking at the final semester. Once qualified, you were entitled to the title of 'doctor'.

Becoming a doctor was only the first of many hazard laden steps for a medical professional. You started with some academic credentialling. There would be specialization and sub-specialization. Completion of academic credentialling was a prerequisite for practice but not a recipe for excellence. But there were enough technically trained people around. Many of them could not get the jobs they wanted. They would flit from job to job or garner few fellowships before slotting into a niche. The art of medicine was long and not everyone enjoyed the travails. Saliba was not fond of blood. She had the self-assured confidence and vivacious exuberance of a natural leader. You needed sharp minds to manage money and men. Saliba felt that she had the vision and flair for management.

The afternoon sun was warm, but with the train's window open and the breeze streaming in, the weather remained bearable. Her friends were already at Wayanad. They would have organized the equipment and maps for the planned adventure. A foray into the reserve forest would be beset with challenges and tinged with danger. It was also true that the transit zone between forest and human encroachments were higher in the risk quotient for animal attacks. Deep in the forests, everyone knew their place. and attacks and aggression reflected the competitive need for food, mates and territory.

Nudging Wayand was dense forest.

Here human intrusions were rare and animals went about their business in natural tranquility. Loss of forest habitat irked the animals and aroused their hostility. Intrusions and counter intrusions of man and animal lead on to the occasional catastrophe. Once you traversed the border zone into the wild, the forest remained pristine, with exotic Flora and Fauna. A short walk from Wayanad town would bring you to a mini township which was the gateway to the reserve forest.

The township itself was small and unpresuming. It was centered around a couple of tourist hotels which provided base camps for the intrepid eco tourist. Solar panels of the hotel roof provided electricity for rooms and for the adjacent roads. From your hotel room you could gaze over the forest with its majestic elephant troupes, gamboling deer and the occasional crouching predator.

Tourists were permitted entry into this

protected forest, only when accompanied by a forest guide. Saliba and her friends were members of the state's eco-protection society. This was a long-awaited forest hike. They had received passes allowing them entry into the beautiful forests unaccompanied. They planned to hike cross-country to Mankadu, a township across the border, in Tamilnadu. The hike would take then five days and then a bus would bring them back to Kochi.

The boy and his parents got off the train at Shornur.   The compartment was emptying now. In an hour, the train would be at kozhikode. Saliba wondered, if this were to be her last trek in Kerala. Her elder brother had already migraited to Australia, after his business school. With his wife and two kids, they stayed in a rambling large house outside Melbourne.   He had been goading Saliba to complete her master's degree from Melbourne University.   Their women's basketball team was iconic. He was confident Saliba would slot in and excel.

There was plenty of room in his house and Saliba was a real hit with her sister-in-law and the kids.

2# The Trekkers Team Up

The train drew up at Kozhikode station. The platform seemed deserted. She was looking for Reena, the other girl in the adventure group. Then Saliba spied them. Her friends were there, near the platform entrance. A sole signalman waving his flag was the only other man around. Saliba stepped on to the platform. Heaving her rucksack across her shoulders, she strolled over. There were four young men and Reena waiting for her.

Reena and Saliba had known each other for mor a year. Reena was a student of biotechnology at the local engineering college. They met each other at a college fest. They soon discovered that they had common interests, concordant political views and compatible culinary tastes. Reena was a self-professed and unapologetic extrovert. Saliba played Basketball with her in the engineering college grounds and had given the girl's team there, useful coaching tips. They had gone out to movies and even attended some political rallies together.

Saliba and Reena were both eco-conservation enthusiasts. They had done a few eco hikes together and had gone snorkeling off the Lakshadeep Islands. Reena was an attractive girl and intensely aware of her sensuality. Her weakness was that she was a little too free with the boys. Saliba was no prude. She was aware of the prudish masochistic pretensions of the Indian male and was cautious in her dealings with the opposite sex. We are all entitled to lead our lives to the standards we set, thought Saliba. She looked at the men in the group. She knew three of them. They were all students.   There was Rahul – a self-professed geek, who liked to unwind on nature trails. Salim and Rashid were from the law college. They were good athletes and good in their studies. Saliba smiled at them. They were good friends to have in a crisis. The fourth man, introduced to her as

Prashant was an NRI. An alumnus of IIT Bombay he had recently finished B school. Reena and he had got to know each other on the net. She had invited him to join them on this trek. He was tall, handsome and looked very physically fit.

"We got all the stuff – said Reena – pointing to the packed Ruck sacks behind. We also managed to procure a clearance from the forest office. They discussed plans as they walked across to the bus station. The bus to Wayanad would be leaving soon. They seemed to be the only passengers. The route to Wayanad was through forest terrain and elephants often strayed into the road. It was an hour's drive to Wayanad. They would disembark a few kilometers away. A short walk would bring them to a mini township from where they would start their hike. The bus conductor cautioned them to stay indoors. Elephants and the occasional tiger menaced the area after sundown. There were a couple of resorts available. The forest had been closed to tourists for six months. They would be the only tenants tonight. They had decided to spend the night at the government tourist bungalow. It was best to start a trek early in the morning.

Their rooms were on the first floor just a monkey swing away from the tree line. Outside, the feeble street lamp, flickered, faded and winked. Saliba slept. She woke up at midnight, confused and wondering where she was. It took a while, for sounds of the forest streaming in through the windows to orient her. There was a faint rumble in the background, she could not decipher. Swinging off the bed she tiptoed to the window. Shimmering moon flakes glittered on lush green leaves outside. She inhaled deeply of the misty enigmatic aroma. She glanced at the fluorescent hands of the wall clock. It would be one soon. She would sleep another three hours. A long day lay ahead.

Saliba woke up well before sunrise. She put her back pack in order and then decided to go down and stroll around town. It was not much of a town. The few locals depended on tourism related gigs for their livelihood. There were two hotel complexes offering eco-tourism packages. Building in this locale involved forest department and tourism board clearances. Both hotels were constructed in a classical Kerala architectural pattern. Both were set on the hill-side overlooking the lush green forest valley below. Behind the buildings, on the other side, were sheer rock cliffs. A water-fall broke the monotony of the rock face. Churned, bubbly, crystal-clear water rumbled a martial melody as it cascaded down the rock and into a shimmering lake. This was the rumble she had heard last night.

Saliba did a few stretches before jogging up and down the central street. It was always better to warm up before getting out on a long trek. After ten minutes she stopped to cool down. A faint pink glow over the horizon heralded the sun's entry. Saliba headed back. When she reached back to the room, Reena was getting ready. She glanced at Saliba in her tracks and raised her eyebrows. Saliba's confidence, resilience and discipline always gave her an inferiority complex.

They had a light breakfast of sandwiches and a cup of tea before setting out. There were enough provisions to last a week. They carried a few bottles of mineral water. Whenever possible, they would refill their water bottles from the mountain streams. Flowing water in the hills was generally safe for consumption. They would also ensure water safety by adding chlorine tablets to any water they collected from the streams before consumption.

3# The Adventure Starts:

They studied the maps one last time. The route charted involved a series of hiking tracks. The tracks were along the hill side, mostly above the tree line. In the depth of the valley, the forest was dense and impassable. They set out with enthusiasm tempered with trepidation. It was still quite dark when they started out. The terrain was unfamiliar. Their eyes soon got used to the dim light. Visibility improved as the walked, despite a fine puff of mist hovering over the hills. Sunlight was slowly peeping in. The hiking path meandered over the mountain side. There was no one else in sight. The ground was moist and in parts, a little soggy. The monsoons were due in a week or two. Pre monsoon sprinkles had green hued brown trees.

They walked carefully. The occasional pre-monsoon deluges could have washed away parts of the path. It was easy to lose one's direction in mountain trails. The slow and sinuous paths could discombobulate one's sense of direction. The secret was in setting course to a prominent geographical landmark. If they strayed off the path, they would find it again if they were headed in the right direction. They had chosen a peak, due east, as a beacon and planned to head for it. Once they reached this point, they would set the next land mark after plotting their course on the map.

Salim was leading the group, with Rashid after him. They had machetes with them which they used to clear the bushes ahead. Rahul walked behind them, he had a map, a compass and another hand-held device which was tethered to a satellite GPS. They were out of the range of mobile telephone towers. Saliba walked after him, binoculars round her neck. She was enjoying the view. A brilliantly painted Malabar parakeet glided across their path and into the forest below. A mountain squirrel looked quizzically at the group as he mooted on a nut. The group stomped the ground as they walked. Snakes could sense vibrations. The thump of boots would alert snakes of their passage. Sensing vibrations of approaching trekkers, most snakes would slither away.

Behind Saliba, Reena and Prashant carried on an animated discussion on Indian Politics and economic policies. "They might as well have discussed politics in the comfort of their homes", thought Saliba. They were missing out on the scenic wonders of God's Own Country. Saliba had paused at places to point to some fascinating spectacle in the scenery or to identify the occasional rare bird to them. Reena and Prashant showed little interest in the spectacular flora. Saliba gave up. The two of them seemed too engrossed in each other to really care about birds and trees.

The group started hiking downhill. They would have to cross a part of the valley to reach the next hill. Mud rivulets made the descend treacherous. A skid could cause them grievous injury. Saliba was glad that she was in her jeans. On many occasions she had to sit and slide down – using her feet and hands as brakes on the muddy slopes. Reena, had worn shorts. She would be getting bruised and dirty.

As they descended into the valley, following the track got increasingly challenging. The forest was dense now. They strayed off the path on more than one occasion. They would then retrace their steps till they found the path again. Even the mountain peak they were heading for, was mostly obscured by trees. The forest was a whole new world. Monkeys jumped from tree to tree, chattering loudly and smattering insults as they followed the trekkers chopping and pushing their way through the invading dense undergrowth. Another month of rain and the forest path would be fully overgrown. Rahul was using his compass now, trying to make sure that they did not lose direction. They had walked for more than six hours by now and were looking for a place to rest a while. It was dark in the forest. The sun was mostly obscured by the leafy curtain above. They were looking for a place to rest. After a while, they could see the greenish glow of sunlight filtering through the foliage. There would be break in the dense overhead canopy. Soon, the group reached a small lake in the clearing. The darkness was less oppressive here. It would be mid-afternoon now. Even here, the sun was still hidden behind a lattice of leaves. Salim and Rashid set about clearing the shrubs to make place for them to rest a while.

The water in the lake was covered with a thin layer of algae, giving it a greenish hue. Below the layer of vegetation, there was clear, cool water. They decided not to drink from this lake. Stagnant water could nurture and culture nasty surprises. Flowing water was safe. Later, they hoped to find a clean mountain stream.

It was a relief taking off the back

packs. They opened and ate some canned peas and then lay in the soft grass. They would rest for an hour and then move on. Reena and Prashant were continuing with their animated political debate. The others had shut their eyes. Saliba decided to walk around the perimeter of the lake. Gnarled tree roots knitted a walkway around the lake. When the rains pumped up the water level many trees growing down would be partially submerged in the lake. She walked over tree roots at the water's edge. She carried a stick with her, broken off from a dried sapling. She walked along, pausing every few minutes to check the lake's depth with the stick or to survey the trees ahead. Layers of rotten leaves made for a grimy lake bed. The mud she stirred up with her stick send surprised frogs skimming away over the water surface. An indignant water snake eyed her crossly before swimming off across the lake.

The far side of the lake was rocky. Here, the tree line was a meter away from the water mark. She could see a few rocks beneath the clear water. Slinging her shoes around her neck she waded into the lake, stepping carefully from rock to rock. The rest of the group was out of sight now. She rolled up her jeans and shirt, washing the mud off her hands, feet and face. The water was so cool and refreshing that she was tempted to remove her clothes and bathe. Unfortunately, she had not carried a towel with her. There was no one to stand guard. If a monkey, ran away with her clothes, while she was bathing, it would be hilariously embarrassing and logistically tragic.

Saliba turned around and walked back to the group. Reena and Prashant were dozing off. Saliba woke Reena up. "There is some clear water at the other end of lake. Why don't you go there and wash up a bit?" Reena looked up groggily. Her legs were caked with mud. She woke Prashant up and mumbled something in his ear. Saliba watched them as they walked off. She decided to rest a bit more. Saliba lay down and closed her eyes.

Her muscles could do with a recharge. There was some brisk walking to be done after they rested. They had to reach the next hill before night fall. Saliba closed her eyes. She must have dozed off for almost half an hour. When she woke up Salim and Rahul were up. Reena and Prashant were not back. Saliba decided to call them back.

She walked round the lake. Her shoes had dried up and she did not want to get them wet again. She walked through the forest now. There was dense barricade of bushes she had to circumvent before reaching the distant rocky shore. She rounded the bushes and stopped in embarrassment. Reena and Prashant had stripped off their clothes and were frolicking and splashing about in the cool water. They paused, awkwardly, on seeing Saliba "Hurry up, - we have to start walking", Saliba turned around and walked back towards the others. She cringed a bit and cursed herself for intruding into Reena's intimacy.

4# A Serendipitous Discovery:

Feeling a little embarrassed, she took a longer route. She wanted to get away from the lake. She walked away from the lakeside and into the forest. The forest was denser here, but there seemed to be some kind of a path. She kept an eye on the lake. If she drifted too deep into the forest, she could get lost. Suddenly Saliba tripped over a stone, lost her balance and fell. She broke her fall, clutching at a rain tree's roots. With an experienced diligence born of years in competitive sports she examined herself. There was mud on her hands and some assorted bruises, but no major injury. She sat on the forest floor- feeling foolish. Abruptly her hands felt something on the forest floor. She cleared away the foliage and found a small wooden box. It had a lock on it. Saliba examined the box. She guessed that it had fallen from some hiker's bag. She walked back to the group, with the box in her hand.   Maybe they would bump into the owner during the hike. If not, they would hand over the box to the nearest police station, when they reached the town. Saliba walked through the forest, back to the lakeside. In a few minutes she reached the group. They could hear voices of Reena and Prashant as they traced the lake perimeter back to base.

Saliba showed the box to the rest of the group. She described her fall and her serendipitous find. Reena and Prashant had also returned. They all clustered around the mysterious box. It was solidly built. The gleaming wooden box had shiny metallic hinges. The lid was secured with a sophisticated lock. Rashid's father ran a jewelry business. He had seen a box like this with his father. They used it to transfer precious stones and expensive jewelry. These boxes were practically indestructible. Opening this box would need two different keys and fingerprint identification.

What did the box hold? They were not

sure. It would be something valuable. They could not fathom how a jewelry box of this nature reached the reserve forest. Saliba decided to carry it in her Ruck Sack. She redistributed some of her food cans and water bottles between the others to make room for the box.

They started out again. Salim and Rashid were in the lead. The forest canopy was dense and green and the forest floor dark. No land marks were visible. The path was overgrown. With the unplanned and inevitable detours around impassably dense shrubbery and rocky mini mountains, progress was laborious and direction maintenance dubious. It seemed very possible that they would go round in circles till the predators of the night descended and devoured them. Reena and Prashant seemed oblivious to the dangers as they again brought up the rear. Saliba could sense that Reena's giggles and their constant chattering was irritating the others.

Their progress through the forest was

painfully slow. They could sense that they were well behind their planned schedule. Rahul's compass was their only guide to the mountain ahead. They plodded on. Salim and Rashid were taking turns with the Machete. It was hard work. After a while Rashid turned to Prashant. Rashid mumbled something about sharing chores and handed him the machete. Reena scowled, but Prashant was game for it. They would all have to pull their weight. Prashant was good as a leader and he tirelessly cut his way through the forest path. Dusk was rolling in fast and they could still not see through the dense tree cover ahead. Saliba was concerned now. It would be unsafe to sleep in the dense forest. They had to reach the hill side soon. Prashant was still pushing on ahead, his rippling, bulging muscles outlined through his sweat soaked shirt.

5# A Tumultuous night:

Suddenly, without warning they were at the mountain's edge. A sheer rock face rose before them. There was no way they could climb this rock face without professional mountain climbing equipment and expertise. Prashant was sure there would be less challenging climbing spots ahead. They would have to walk on till they found an easier place, where they could start their ascend. There was no path here. Hopping from rock to rock and cutting through shrubbery they moved on. They had strayed off the path a bit. Landmarks could reorient them. In the dark depths of this valley, there were none. They would need to the panoramic view from the mountain top to plan the next day's route.

The sheer rock face seemed to mock them. Reena's suggestion that they try to spend the night up a tree was dismissed as impractical. There were no suitable climbable trees. Besides, leopards who frequented these forests were good climbers too. They were getting exhausted. Luck favored them. The sheer cliff soon gave way to a hillside pock marked with scattered boulders. There was the semblance of a path leading obliquely up the hillside. Going was tough but they were making progress. There were rocks to be climbed over and some slippery patches. They started to climb. Saliba had some experience in rock climbing. She managed the climb easily. Prashant had dropped behind to help Reena. He was carrying both their ruck sacks. The dense forest was behind them soon. It was darker now, but the group kept climbing. The sun had set now, but there was enough moon light to move on.

The benevolent moon was in a hurry to light up the hills. She was already halfway up the evening sky. It would be a moonlit night. The trekkers were tired. They reached a flat ground beneath the final peak and decided to camp there. Salim and Rahul organized a bonfire. They had gathered dry wood enroute. They were well prepared. Rashid had a small bottle of kerosene with him. Splashing kerosene of the dried twigs they started a fire. They had cleared dried leaves and shrubs from around the fire. It would be an ecological disaster it they started a forest fire.

The flames danced in the cool night breeze. Grass around was moist and the fire was unlikely to spread. They rolled out their sleeping bags around the burning embers. They settled down for a well-earned night's rest. One by one they fell asleep.

Saliba lay down looking at the night sky. A few ominous rain clouds played hide and seek with the moon. A few of the brighter stars peeked through the web of moon beams. Below them, in the valley, they could hear the sounds of a forest coming alive. Excited monkeys chattered their alarm as they spotted a predator. A flock of birds fluttered up into the air in alarm as a snake slithered close.

Saliba's eyes closed on their own accord. She slid into a well-earned slumber. A woman's whisper roused Saliba. She drifted into wakefulness. From the corner of her eye, she saw Reena waking up Prashant. Saliba kept her eyes shut and pretended to sleep. Soon Prashant and Reena were up and with conspiratorial glances at the other sleeping campers tiptoed off into the darkness. Saliba hoped, that they would not go too far away. She slept off again.

Saliba woke up hearing voices. The voices were rough and the language they spoke was unfamiliar. Saliba felt intense dread and fear. Her consternation was worse than any she had encountered in her life. She opened he eyes and closed them again, quaking with fear. A group of men, all of them armed with sophisticated looking guns, had surrounded the campers. Saliba closed her eyes and pretended to be asleep. She tried to convince herself that it was a bad dream. She would wake up, back in her hostel and marvel at the lucidity of the nightmare.

A hard boot got her on her hip. "Get Up" growled the man who had kicked her. He had raised his boot to stomp her again. Saliba scrambled trembling and terrified to her feet. She looked around. One of the gangsters held her by the collar of her shirt. Others in the group were also getting the same treatment. Salim must have put up a fight, his nose was bloody and he stood crouched over, holding his lower abdomen. Their assailants were unshaven. They were young men. Their sadistic demeanor suggested a propensity to violence. The men wore camouflage jackets and carried guns slung casually over their shoulders.

Saliba realized that the men were not locals. She discerned that the group was conversing with one another in Hindi, with a Punjabi slang. Saliba looked around for Reena and Prashant.   They were nowhere to be seen. She hoped that they would escape and get help. The men noticed her glances. One of them came to her. The man was rough and bearded and wore a red scarf round his neck. He grabbed her by her hair. Pointing to the two unclaimed sleeping bags he asked, "Where are they?". He was shaking her, almost wrenching her hair off. Her neck was hurting and she almost lost consciousness. Saliba held up her hand – feigning helpless ignorance. A blow rent her reeling. Rohit stepped forward to protect her, but was knocked senseless by a rifle butt.

There were shouted commands. The men fanned out in all directions searching for the missing campers. Two of them stayed back, herding the prisoners into a huddle. Saliba and the boys were ordered to kneel down. The boys were totally cowed down. Saliba was the only one with a covert sparkle in her eyes. The sparkle was tinged with raw apprehension. She was totally at their mercy. They were miles away from civilization. If the men brutalized her, the sparkle in her eyes and in her life would be extinguished for eternity.

They stayed on their knees, utterly helpless, in a tight frightened group, by the campfire. One of the men was searching their bags. Water bottles, cans and spare clothes tumbled out of Salim and Rashid's Bags. The other man watched over the group of prisoners, occasionally spitting in their direction in a show of contempt. The man with the red scarf was opening Saliba's Ruck Sack now. The mysterious box   she found on the forest floor tumbled out. There was a yell of surprise from the man. He lifted the box up carefully and examined it. Their guard too was staring open mouthed at the locked box.   They all flocked around, examining the box.

6# Saliba Escapes:

Saliba saw her chance. Springing to her feet, she ran for the trees. She had almost reached the tree line when the man realized what was happening. There was a shout from the man with the red scarf. Another man, who had been standing guard, turned and fired his gun. The bulled missed Saliba by inches as she dived into the bushes. The boys did not move. They knew that if they moved a whisker, they would be killed. The man was firing wildly into the bushes. If the guards chased Saliba into the forest, it would give the boys a window to escape. The guards were however professional. They had been discombobulated by the discovery of the box in Saliba's bag. The shock and surprise had allowed her the chance to escape. The men were professional soldiers. There would be no more lapses. They would not leave the prisoners till some of the search party returned.

Saliba sat, crouched behind a tree trunk. She picked up a stone and threw it down the cliff, where it clattered down the rocks. The man immediately started firing in the direction of the sound. Saliba ran now, dodging behind trees and bushes, desperately trying to put as much distance as possible from the clearing. Whenever she saw a stone, she would throw it towards the cliff. There was a burst of gunfire. The man could not see her. He was firing his gun blindly in the direction of the sound.

Saliba was soon deep in the forest, but she kept going. As long as some of them were free, the men would probably not kill their prisoners. Saliba kept moving for another 15 minutes and then stopped. There were footsteps behind. Someone was following her. She had heard a twig snap. The footsteps behind stopped. No bullets were fired. Whoever was following her, wanted her alive. Saliba hid behind a tree. The footsteps chasing her stopped. Saliba picked up a stone. Holding it firmly raised to strike she moved round the tree, ready to strike. Suddenly a strong arm snaked around her neck and closed her mouth. The other arm had pinned her arms to the side. She could feel her captor's rippling muscles as he squeezed her body into submission. She tried to fight free. She could hardly breathe. The attacker waited till her struggles subsided before he whispered in her ear, "Saliba, it is me' Prashant".

Prashant released his grip. Saliba was still leaning against him. She slid down to the forest floor, only partially conscious. He laid her out on the ground. Her pulse was feeble. Slowly, the pulse got stronger. Saliba's eyes opened. He told her what happened. Prashant and Reena had just settled down behind a clump of bushes when they heard footsteps and hushed voices. He had pulled Reena deeper into the brush and asked her to hide there. He had then followed the men as they circled the camp. Unarmed, there was little he could do, as the men roughed up

Saliba and the boys. He, like Saliba had surmised that they would not kill them if they suspected that some members of the group were still free.

Prashant planned to escape through the forest and get to the nearest police station. He got back to Reena and explained what he had seen. The men were terrorists or part of some sophisticated smuggling ring. The weapons they carried and their efficient ruthlessness seemed to suggest the former. The box was an enigma. Locked up in the box was the answer to many questions.

He was trying to get Reena to escape with him when they heard voices. Two of the terrorists, their guns swinging in short arcs were headed their way. Prashant pulled Reena after him behind a boulder. Then Reena panicked. Trembling with fear, she stepped out of the bush with her hands up. One of the men hit Reena on the head with his

Rifle. and then slung her unconscious body over his shoulder before heading toward the camp. Prashant was preparing to charge them, when he heard shouts from the camp and saw Saliba running into the forest. He had followed her.

The two of them kept walking as soundlessly as possible. The more distance they could put between themselves and the gunmen, the safer they would be.
It was almost day break when the two of them paused to rest. They crawled up between the roots of a huge tree and lay down. Saliba's head rested on Peasant's muscled arm. She felt safe and secure with Prashant. Her eyes closed and she was soon fast asleep. Prashant looked at the sleeping girl. She was beautiful. Her face was angelic and was glowing with natural radiance even after all the danger and misadventure they had been through. Turning to her, with his arm thrown across her sleeping figure and his nose nuzzling her hair he too slept. He knew the challenges ahead. They both

needed the sleep and the rest. The sun was snooping upon them, peeping between the tree tops when they woke up. Saliba blushed a bit when she realized that Prashant had woken up a while ago but had not moved, letting her sleep on, on his arm.

They freshened up and took stock of the situation.   To try and get back to Wayanad was fraught with menace. Irate armed baddies were combing the forests behind them. The forest was in a valley ringed by hills. They decided to continue the course they had charted earlier. They had planned to head for the nearest township across the forest. That route was still their best bet at reaching civilization and help. They would have to trek through the forest. If they climbed up for a clearer track, they would be spotted.

The hill they had climbed yesterday was to their right. If they continued walking through the forest, they would reach a ring of hills. Over the hills ahead was the township they had headed for. Saliba had a suggestion. Heading straight for the township was probably not a good idea. The gang would have the groups route plans from their prisoners. The armed group could lay an ambush for Saliba and Prashanth before they could contact anyone. It would be safer to take a detour. Prashant suggested that they could head for a road and solicit a lift in a passing vehicle. They could stop at the nearest police station and get a rescue effort organized for their friends who were prisoners. Prashant estimated that if they kept going straight, they should reach a highway about 80 kilometers. They would have to walk through the forest for two days at least before they reached the road. With detours and the need for stealth, their passage could be longer. The route was fraught with danger. The forest was dense and almost impassable in places. They could encounter elephant herds or predators. Their progress through the dense undergrowth where no paths were available would be painfully slow. They had no food with them. All they had was a quart of water in Prashant's hip flask.

Saliba and Prashanth kept walking. They communicated mostly in sign language and tried to be as stealthy as possible. Barring rustles, bustles, bird calls and monkey chatter, there were no ominous sounds. There was no sign of any pursuit. Every couple of hours they would settle in a safe patch and rest. They discussed evolving options. Prashant and Saliba worried about their friend's fate. Prashant was sure that the prisoners would be kept alive as long as the two of them were free. Prisoners could be used as hostages or bargaining chips.

Armed gangsters were the last thing the group of hikers expected to encounter in a desolate stretch of dense forest. They had not confided to anyone on the trekking plan. No one had their route details. Mobile phones with them had run out of charge. Anyway, there was no connectivity in the forest.

Being in a group they had been overtly confident of safety. Four of the group were now captives. They were danger and even if they were kept alive they would potentially be hostages. Saliba and Prashant were free.

They had to strike out and get help. No one would miss them for a week at least. There was no one who would mount a search effort or raise an alarm. Prashant kept trying to guess who the bandits were. These were not Naxalites. They were professional soldiers on a mission. What was the mission? Knowing their antecedents could provide insights into their motivation and vulnerabilities. Saliba told Prashant about the men's reaction on discovering the box in her bag. If she had remained in captivity she would have been tortured and molested during interrogation. The men would never accept her story that she had discovered the box accidentally in the mud of the forest floor. Prashant was sure that the box held some vital link in the mystery.

They wondered what mission the men were on. They were too well equipped to be ordinary dacoits or robbers. Had they stumbled upon a smuggling ring. But what would a smuggling ring be doing, operating so far inland? What was there in the box? There were too many questions and great danger. Saliba was hungry and thirsty now. It was 24 hours since they last had a meal. The water pouch strapped to Prashant's hip was empty now. She looked at Prashant. He was wearing a stoic yet brave expression. She knew that despite his brave front, Prashant was suffering too.

It was quite late in the afternoon, when they chanced upon a mountain stream. Greedily they drank of the sparkling clear water. There was a rocky pond to the side of the stream into which water gurgled from some underground reservoir. Saliba made Prashant turn around as she bathed in the pond. Prashant had disappeared into the forest and he now returned with a ripe

Jackfruit. He broke the kernel on a rock and together they ate the delicious fruit. Saliba felt much stronger now. Prashant fashioned a spear for himself with his penknife. He made a smaller club for Saliba. The weapons would be of little use against a major predator. However, it restored in the duo a sense of control. They decided to follow the stream's course.   At least it would lead somewhere. Besides, they would have access to water and possibly food enroute. The danger was that they could encounter animals coming for the water who might find them a threat or consider them palatable.

It was growing dark now and Saliba wondered, where they would sleep. The sun had set and the moon was in hiding behind a dense shroud of cloud. They followed the water, guided by the gentle crackling of the stream, as it meandered through the forest. Prashant assessed that they were heading south easterly. Every couple of hours they would take a break. With water and nutrition their resilience and strength had been restored. They kept drinking of the stream's water. Intermittently they would stop and share some more of the Jackfruit, Prashant had carried along.

The moon emerged again and they could walk faster now. They slept again on a patch of clear grass by the stream's edge. They kept each other warm and safe through the cold dark night. Animals of the forest left them alone. The early rays of the sun woke them up. Ahead of them was a clearing and they headed for it. They were outside the tree line now. A furlong ahead of them was a large lake, its waters placid. A platoon of elephants drank from the lake's shallow waters, a short distance away. A deer peeped at them and then cantered away to join its herd. They were just about to step out into the open sand, when Prashant held up his hand. He steadied Saliba who stumbled. They stood still, their hearts pounding in synchrony. They could hear men's voices coming closer through the forest. Had their pursuers outmaneuvered them?

Saliba and Prashant hid behind the bushes. They could hear the stomp of boots as a troop of men approached. This was another group. Saliba and Prashant studied them. They were all young men, in camouflage outfits and jungle boots. They marched with the loping easy stride of elite commandos. All of them carried dull gleaming automatic weapons, which they held poised in trained easy familiarity. These were not the men who had attacked them, but they seemed to be of the same group. Saliba and Prashant stayed still and remained concealed as the group went past them. The troop seemed to be returning after a night of patrolling. Snippets of the group's conversation wafted down to Saliba and Prashant. There was some talk of four intruders being caught. Two more were hidden in the forest and would be rounded up as soon as they popped their noses out of the forest. Saliba grimaced. The men were right. It would take Saliba and Prashanth all their ingenuity and loads of luck if they were to bypass the patrols and escape.

Prashant and Saliba watched as the men loped around the lake giving wide berth to the elephant herd. Where were they headed?

7# Terror Headquarters:

The men were now heading away from the lake and into the tree line. Saliba and Prashanth decided to follow the group. It would give them insights into the group's ethos. It was possible that they could find their friends. Once you knew your enemy, you could use his resources. Would they have to follow the men through the forest to find out where they were headed? Sunlight was slowly flooding the valley. They could see better now. Saliba spotted it first. On the far side of the lake, through the tree line, they could see, what looked like a sprawling Forest Bungalow. The construct was of gleaming wood and granite. In all probability, this forest retreat was built by the British as a holiday home. Sloping tiled roofs and traditional designs proffered the building a colonial splendor.

Prashant and Saliba watched as the group walked around the lake and towards the forest bungalow. They could see white smoke emanating from the chimneys of the Bungalow. Over the quite cackle and bustle of the forest, a soft hum of machinery could be heard. From the front of the building, a motorable mud track snaked its war into the dark forest. The lake drained into a wide river which Saliba and Prashant could now see in the distance. They realized they were way off their original route. This was the Pookot lake. The river would be draining into the Cauvery.

"We seem to have stumbled on the group's head- quarters". Said Prashant testily. The option of escaping to the National Highway and soliciting a lift was fading. They were off course. Plans would need to be recalibrated considering evolving events. The serendipitous discovery of the epi-center of unknown evil brought forward danger and opportunity. It was Saliba who suggested that they check out if Reena and the boys were being held prisoners in the bungalow. Prashant looked at her with admiration. He had been mulling over this option but had demurred considering the danger. These were trained armed men they were dealing with. They would have little hesitation to shoot unwelcome intruders. Their proclivity to violence was apparent. Yet Saliba's initiative bolstered his courage. He had never met a woman with such soft strength and sensuous resilience. Together they planned out a strategy.

Keeping themselves concealed behind the tree line, they followed the armed group. As they grew closer to the house, Prashant raised his hand in a gesture of caution. There would be a look out posted somewhere. The group ahead was near the building. Saliba and Prashant saw the group pause close to the house. Suddenly Saliba spotted the look out. He was in a tree house a hundred yards from the bungalow. The group leader seemed to exchange some pleasantries with him before moving on. Saliba and Prashant edged closer through the forest. They could see the bungalow clearly. It was constructed of granite and teak wood. A few stone pillars supported a series of wooden platforms on which the house was built. A ramp led down from the bungalow down to the lake. There was jetty in the lake and a boat was moored there. There was a small boathouse by the jetty. A light flickered within. A sentry would be on duty to guard the boat.

They shifted their attention back to the bungalow. A fair fervent bit of engineering effort seemed to have been done there recently. There were stacks of cement and assorted pipes, tubes and wires In a makeshift enclosure. Saliba remembered reading about a forest guest house which was being converted into a hotel. The hotel was to be inaugurated during the Onam festival, which was a few months away.

There was a moat around the bungalow. This was designed to keep elephants out. A tickling stream ran through the moat.

Someone had bifurcated and harnessed a natural mountain stream on its way to the lake. Rocks jutting out from the walls provided potential toe and finger holds. They looked at each other. The moat could be crossed. The sentry was a deterrent. Beyond the moat there was a lush green lawn. Ringing the house were pine trees. These and some creeping vines would keep the house walls cool in summer.

Reaching the bungalow without being seen and shot or captured seemed improbable. Any one crossing the moat would be seen by the tree house sentry. Prashant was sure that surveillance cameras scanned the grounds. They had to look for a weak spot of vulnerability in the surveillance system. Saliba and Prashant stayed behind the trees as they walked, crouching, around the moat. They were looking for a blind spot in the tree sentry's zone of surveillance. Suddenly Prashant stopped. He pointed straight ahead. Another tree house and sentry provided on observation post on the opposite side. There was no way they could approach the house without being seen.

Saliba pulled Prashant deeper into the forest. There was some commotion coming from near the first sentry post. They could hear the stomp of boots and muffled curses. Another group was approaching. They had with them the boys and Reena. The boy's hands had been tied behind but Reena's hands were free. The armed men who had attacked their camp were irate, rough and vicious. They prodded the prisoners along with their rifle butts, abuse and the occasional sharp kick. Fortunately – no one seemed to be severely hurt. Saliba and Prashant watched, as their friends were herded and hustled into the bungalow. Lights came on in the bungalow. A window on the first floor was opened and then closed again. Saliba guessed that this was where the captives would be held.

It was growing dark. Saliba looked up. Clustered storm clouds were hovering overhead. The drum beat of distant peals of thunder was drawing nearer.   In the distance, they could see pillars of rain conglomerating.   The subdued whistle of cyclonic water whirls became a growl as walls of rain rolled and drew closer. Over the rumble of the approaching storm- they heard the roar of a vehicle. A jeep was driving up, along the jungle path. It stopped near the bungalow and a tall bearded man in a Pathani outfit dismounted. There was an aura of sanguine power emanating from him. He was flanked followed by two armed guards. Some of the men in the house came out to receive him.   The tall man was obviously some out of a leader. From the deference they showed him his authority was apparent.

The rain come down on them in torrents. The lookout on the tree top was huddled beneath a cape. Visibility was low.   They could hardly see a few feet in front of their faces. There was a bolt of thunder, so close and intense that they thought they had been incinerated. A lighting rod on the Bungalow roof glowed red and turned white as megavolts of heavenly energy ignited the cables. The house lights lit up in extreme brilliance and then were off. Fuses had tripped. Saliba and Prashant appreciated this window of opportunity. "Let's go" she said. Holding hands, so as not to lose each other. They scampered down into the moat and climbed up the opposite wall. Dusting off their hands, they sprinted for the bungalow. They had to get beyond the pines before the lights came on. Saliba prayed that no further lightning flashes would illuminate them and blow their cover of darkness.

8# The Lion's Den

Luck was in their favor. Saliba and Prashanth reached the building undetected. They were looking for a place to hide before starting any exploration. There was a partially constructed area behind the house. Saliba and Prashant hid behind the walls. They were soaked and muddy. They had the element of surprise on their side. However. there was no concrete plan. A vague yet fervent desire to free their friends and escape to safety had taken precedence over any quest to unravel the mysteries of the bungalow. Yet, both were interlinked. They had stumbled on a mystery and an operation that put them far beyond their depth.

For now, they were safe. Unless there was a deliberate organized search, no one would find them. The storm passed as quickly as it had started, revealing patches of purple sky. Dusk was settling in. A generator had been started and lights came on in the bungalow. Beams of two powerful search lights punched holes in the darkness and strategically placed fluorescent porch lights soon lit up the grounds around.

Saliba and Prashant kept clear of the search lights probing beam. They were drenched and cold and held each other close to keep warm. As the darkness settled in, Saliba and Prashant   inched around the parapet. There was a window ahead, with wide tinted glass panes, glowing with pearly fluorescence. A conference of sorts seemed to be going on inside. The tall man, who had come by jeep was seated at the head of the table on brilliantly polished gleaming teak wood chair. A dozen armed men stood in a semi circle before him in alert deferential respect. On the table, in front of them, lay a dozen boxes. These boxes were exact replicates of the one Saliba had picked up from the forest floor.

The leader was inspecting one box very

carefully. He seemed to be ascertaining that no one had opened it. He seemed satisfied and handed box back to a guard. There were twelve locked boxes in all. Their content remained a mystery. Saliba and Prashant walked along the ledge carefully. The men were focused on some maps they had on the table. Unless someone stared at the window their silhouettes would not be seen. The parapet ringed the house. They stepped over a humming air conditioning unit.

The window of the next room was barred. There were lights shining inside. This could be where the prisoners were being held. Through a crack in the window, they peeked inside. They were right. Their friends sat on the floor. They looked scared and exhausted. The boy's hands were tied behind their backs. Reena sat on the floor in the corner of the room. Her hair was disheveled and her blouse was torn. She was not trussed up like the others. There was an armed sentry in the room. He sat with his feet on a table openly ogling Reena.

Suddenly a door opened and the tall man who had come in the jeep walked in. A troop of bodyguards followed him. The sentry jumped up from his chair. He retrieved the cap he had tossed casually on the table and wore it. His discomfiture was obvious. He had not expected his commander to walk in. All eyes were on the commander. Would he summarily execute his prisoners? Prashant and Saliba could see him better now. He was a tall well built man. He stood ramrod straight as he surveyed the prisoners. The boys shivered in their corner. Renna felt strangely reassured by his presence. The man radiated strength. Yet, his melancholy eyes and aquiline features proffered him a vulnerability which was perceptible and unique. He was a man who had been forged in a crucible of violence and pain. There was a scar on his face which stretched from below his right eye almost to his lip. He looked over the motley group with benevolent empathy and gave instructions to his men.

He turned to the guard who was sweating profusely. "Give them chairs and let them sit at the table". His voice was resonant yet restrained. He spoke with authority which brooked no dissent or discussion. He looked at Reena his eloquent eyes brimming with compassion and understanding. He could sense her discomfiture and the guard's intentions. "Do you want to stay here or will you come with me to my house", He asked Reena. Reena was teary in her gratitude. "I will come with you". She was sure that is she stayed on as a prisoner in the room, the guard would molest her.

9# In the Bungalow:

One of the men helped Reena to her feet. They left the room. The guard returned to his chair looking disappointed. The main door of the bungalow was opening. A driver had started the jeep. A guard opened the front door for their leader to get in. Two of his body guards, along with Reena, got into the back. The jeep took off and then stalled in the mud. There was a curse from the leader. The armed men ran down to give a hand as the vehicle's tires whirled in shrill futility, spraying mud in all directions. The driver cut the engine. The bungalow door was unguarded and all attention was focused on the jeep. Someone ran to get wooden planks. They were pushing the jeep on to the planks. The jeep engine was started again.

Saliba signaled to Prashant. This was a

chance for them to enter the bungalow. The bungalow was a large building. There would be places inside where they could hide. Once inside they could have a chance to rescue their friends during the night. They might also get clues to unravel the mystery of the boxes. Saliba and Prashant lowered themselves down from the ledge. Hiding behind the trees they moved towards the open door. There was no one watching the door. They sneaked in in, just as the jeep took off. The men would be returning now. They ran into the first room. They could hear footsteps of the men returning to the door. There were steps leading down into the basement. They scampered down the steps, desperately looking for a place to hide. They found themselves in a dark room. Their eyes slowly adapted to the dark. There was a heavy door straight ahead.

Tentatively they pushed the door open. The dull grow of a night lamp showed that they were in a store room of sorts. Drums, looking like wine barrels were stacked against the wall. The drums were painted white and had spine chilling Biohazard warnings stamped on them. At the other end of the room was a steel door with a reinforced glass pane. Prashant tiptoed across. There was no one around. Prashant tried to open the door. It was locked and would require some biometric identity verification for opening. He called Saliba. They peeked in through the glass. Inside, they could see what appeared to be a laboratory of sorts. As they watched, a man wearing Biohazard protective gear including a mask with a breathing apparatus emerged from on one of the side rooms adjacent to the corridor. He was at the wheel of a electric golf cart fitted with a forklift and a robotic arm. He turned the cart and was coming toward the door.

Prashant and Saliba looked desperately for a place to hide. They dove for cover behind the stack of barrels just as the man reached the door. They waited with bated breath as the heavy door slid open powered by an electric motor. There was hum from the stack as a conveyor belt whirled. A barrel was tipped on to the belt by an unseen mechanical lever. As they watched, the man in the cart manipulated a set of levers operating his cart's robotic arm. He loaded the barrel in his trolley and turned towards the laboratory. The door slid open remotely and the man drove in. The door slid shut.

Meanwhile, they could hear voices from upstairs. They listened carefully. The front door had opened again. From receding footsteps and fading voices they surmised that men were trooping out. Saliba heaved a sigh of relief. Prashant smiled. If there were only a couple of guards left back within the house, they would have a chance to rescue the boys.

The jeep, with Reena in it was being driven along a mud track through the forest a little distance from the lakes edge. It was dark in the forest but shards of moonlight flashed incisive glimpses into the forest's ethos. Herds of deer gamboled away on hearing the jeep's rumble. Monkeys chattered. Flocks of birds rose into the air from their perches before settling down again. Red eyes, glowing in the glare of the jeep's headlights peeked out at them from the dark recesses of the jungle around. The driver mumbled something about a lone tusker in the vicinity. The Leader did not seem unduly perturbed. His presence and confidence made Reena feel secure.

Reena was relieved to be out of the bungalow. The sentry who had stood guard over them had frightened her. If she had been at the bungalow, she would not have been safe. The leader of the group, looked like a man of character. He must be in his early forties, thought Reena'. His features, built and complexion, suggested that he was probably of Pathan stock. With his beaked nose, piercing eyes and square jaw he could have been a movie star, if it were not for the cruel scar across his face. His body guards and the car driver were young muscular men.

They obviously held him in deep reverence – not even venturing to speak in his presence. Reena felt strangely reassured and wanted to speak to him. Yet, she felt, she could not take the liberty. He might consider it an affront.

Prashant stealthily crept up the stairs. The front door was closed. He could hear voices inside. There was still a group of men around in the house. But they too seemed to be preparing to leave. Someone was coming towards the door. Prashant climbed down the stairs softly. The stairwell was dark and he would not be observed. The man had opened the front door. Other footsteps could be heard. A troop seemed to be moving out on Patrol. He waited till the crunch of the Jungle boots exited the foyer. Only a couple of guards remained in the house. The Front door closed again.

Tentatively he opened the door to the store room. The room was dimly lit by light filtering through the glass panes from the laboratory complex. He looked around. It was obvious that the basement laboratory was key to the enigma. If they could get a peek in, the mystery would be unveiled. There was the constant rumble of machinery from somewhere beneath the house. Somewhere beneath the laboratory complex was a generator unit. The stacked Biohazard labelled barrels suggested some kind of Biotechnology venture.

Prashant looked around the room. He could see Saliba, hiding behind the barrel rack. He realized that they would need a better and darker place to hide if someone were to venture into the room. The technician in the protective suit had not been very observant or they would have been spotted when he came to change barrels.

The generators were chugging one floor below them. The main entrance to the generator room would be accessible by road. Prashant guessed that there would be an emergency or maintenance entrance to the generator room somewhere. He soon found what he was looking for. There was a wooden trap door concealed beneath the stairs. He opened it and peered inside. The sound of the generator was suddenly louder. The trapdoor was the emergency exit. Below them was the generator room. Prashant guessed that there would be another entrance where tankers would be docking to replenish generator fuel reserves.

Beneath the open trap door was a wooden ladder. Prashanth waved to Saliba. She ran softly across the room. Saliba climbed down the ladder. 'Look for a light switch," Prashant urged her. He
kept the trap door open, letting some light filter in. He kept an eye on the laboratory door. He would ease the trapdoor shut if someone opened the trapdoor. Saliba found the switch near the bottom of the stairs. She switched on the lights. The generator room would be locked from the outside and they could hide here.

10# A Romantic Interlude:

Prashant gently closed the door and joined her. They were in a basement cum store room. A large and surprisingly sophisticated generator hummed effectively in the center. Barrels of diesel were stocked in a net row against the walls. There were pipes going out, with exhaust fans providing ventilation. Behind the barrels there was a strong smell of fuel. But on the opposite wall near the ventilation pipe there seemed to be a maintenance ledge. They climbed up to the ledge. To one side was change area with a couple of freshly pressed dungarees hanging from wall hooks. The fuel handlers would be changing into work clothes here. There would be no gas tankers coming in at night. Prashant and Saliba could lie there and not be seen unless there was a systematic search. even if people come into the room. Saliba watched, while Prashant crept back and switched off the light. He groped his way back to the ledge. Their clothes were wet with sweat and mud. They helped each other undress and later to ease into the dungarees. Prashant lay down next to Saliba. They would rest for a couple of hours.

Reena had dosed off in the jeep in spite of the intimidating terrain. The men had treated her with respect unlike earlier, when she had been poked and prodded by her captors. She opened her eyes as the jeep slowed and then stopped. The head lamps were doused. They were in some sort of a clearing in the forest. Reena looked around. The jeep had drawn to a halt in front of a Giant Banyan tree. A rope ladder dangled down. She looked up. There was a light coming through the leaves. Reena first thought that it was a bright full moon. She looked up again. Nestled high amongst the branches was a small tree house. It was supported on wooden stilts and propped up against a rock cliff behind. A mountain stream that trickled down the rock face, had been diverted to give water to the house.

A petromax lantern was burning in the house. There was another small hut on a ledge in the rock face at the far end of the clearing. A guard had emerged from the hut in camouflage fatigues. He stood ramrod straight as the leader dismounted from the jeep. One of the guards held open the door for Reena. Legs weary with fatigue, she too got off the jeep.

The leader spoke to her directly for the first time. "This is my house – will you like to come up with me or would you rather stay here with my men?". Reena did not hesitate. "I will come with you". Reena had no desire to spend the night with a bunch of boisterous guards. She climbed the rope ladder as the leader held it steady. He followed her to the hut, drawing up the ladder behind them.

The tree house was sparsely but tastefully furnished. There was a couch and a few chairs on one side and a bed on the other. A bamboo curtain portioned off a small toilet which had water from mountain stream flowing through. There was a prayer mat on the floor of the main room. In one corner of the room was an arms cupboard. An assortment of Rifles and handguns shared space with a silver sword and a commando dagger. Next to gun cupboard was a stacked bookshelf.

The man waved her to a chair and then sat facing her "My name is Khalil. I apologize to you for all the discomfort. You must be wondering what sinister secret you have stumbled upon". Abdullah spoke with sincerity and clarity as Reena listened spell bound. "A Billion Years ago there was big bang. Out of nothingness emerged alternative universes of negativity and positivity. Matter and anti-matter, good and evil, promise and peril. The rapidly expanding universe propelled by the positive forces of the universe are reined in by negativity and evil. The story of human civilization has been crafted by a few great men", he continued. Reena was not listening to his words. She was in thrall of his voice and intensely aware of his presence. Her fragile vulnerability evoked a deep compassion in Khalil. He continued his tirade. "The social balances, which we take for granted today were forged by human sinew and seasoned with blood and tears. The French revolution, the evolution of China, the emancipation of slaves, the list is endless. Great leaders have rallied the oppressed against the Tzars of subjugation. Today we are on the threshold of another upheaval".

There was a crackle of a radio in the background. Khalil excused himself and picked up a receiver. He was going orders to someone now. His voice was crisp, precise and decisive. There was something brewing. Reena knew that she should try to listen. That would help her plan a survival strategy for herself and her friends. Yet, it all seemed of little consequence, weighed against the gravity of his concepts. Her captors animal magnetism and surreal charm were all encompassing and overpowering.

In a flash of rationality Reena realized that Khalil was some sort of a terrorist leader spinning a shibboleth of delusions. She had also figured out, by now that he was orchestrating some murder and mayhem. She realized too that she and her friends would not be allowed to go free. They would probably be killed. The transient lucidity of thought and logic She was shaken by imminent danger to herself and her friends. was transient and logic receded. She was drenched and deluded again by pervasive emotions. There was fear and dread. Yet, she was moved by the man's charisma. There was an undeniable logic behind his cruel machinations.

Khalil turned to Reena "You can sleep on the couch". He told her. She sat on one of the chairs and watched him as he knelt on the prayer mat and said his prayers. He disappeared into the bathroom. When he came out, he had changed from his camouflage into a toga of sorts. She watched him as he lay on the bed and in a minute – his eyes were shut.

There was a towel and a kaftan kept for her in the room. She walked around his bed to and into the toilet. She stripped her clothes off for a bath. A sprinkler head attached to a Bamboo rod made a delectable shower. The sparkling clean water was soothing. Her skin sizzled in the cascading mountain stream. Reena washed her soggy clothes and toweled herself. She danced her fingers down her body, lingering over the bruises. Shaking out the kaftan, she slid into it. The shimmering silk cascaded reluctantly down her curves. In spite of the fear and her bruises, she felt more alive than she had ever been before. The kaftan was sexy, soft and comfortable. She rinsed out her clothes and hung them up to dry. Softly, she paddled out of the bath, her kaftan caressing her body. The sofa looked comfortable. She could do with some sleep.

She paused by Khalil's bed. He seemed to have no fear of her at all, as he slept defenseless. He looks like a God, she thought to herself. Khalil lay immobile and seemed to be barely breathing. Had he died? Reena experienced a sudden surge of panic. She put out her hand over his face to check if he were breathing. She felt his body flushing in arousal. He moved easily, catching her hand in his. Reena could hardly breathe. They froze – looking into each other's eyes – aglow and ablaze in an incandescent tableau. He gently pulled her to bed beside him and kissed her. Then they were swept away in a wave of passion, their bodies and breaths fusing in perfect undulant harmony.

Later – they lay without speaking. Reena closed her eyes, nestled in his powerful arms and slept.

It would have been past midnight when Reena woke up. Subconsciously she snuggled up closer. Her soft succulent lips traced and roamed the magnificent male who had possessed her body and ransomed her soul. He smiled as she rode him in a futile quest for dominance before gasping in abject surrender once again.

11# Prashanth strikes:

Saliba woke up disoriented.   For a minute she could not remember where she was. She sat up with a start. Prashant was sitting close, watching her and smiling. He kissed her as she opened her eyes. "You wait here", he whispered. "I will scout the area and be back." Prashant went up the stairs and softly pushed open the trap door. He looked around. The room above seemed deserted and the laboratory door was closed. He closed the trapdoor silently. He decided to check out the bungalow. Silently and with intense alertness, he went carefully up the steps. The front door was closed and possibly locked. He tiptoed to the door of the conference room. His heart hammering, he twisted the handle and eased the door open.

The furniture was as he remembered it from the night before. He looked around.

The heavy table and sofas would offer some concealment if the front door opened and someone came in to investigate. A night light was burning, but the room was deserted. Hugging the walls and keeping away from the windows he headed for the inner room where their companions were held captive. The door to the inside room was ajar. He could hear sounds of someone moving inside. Prashant heaved a sigh of relief. The prisoners were still there. As the boys were tied up, he guessed there would be limited security.

There were no voices heard. Prashant remembered. The boys had their mouths taped. A rhythmic grunt could be heard. Someone was snoring. Prashant crept up carefully and peeped in through the door. With the windows shut, only shards and flickers of light peeped in through chinks in the window panes. He could see the sentry now. A Loud snore emanating from the guard startled and unsettled him. The sentry was sleeping on a chair with his back to the door.

There was an empty bottle of beer on the table in front of him. The room was dark. He would make out the silhouettes of the three boys lying trussed up and blind folded in a corner. The leader's instructions to seat them comfortably had been ignored.

Prashant looked around for a weapon. He would have to overpower and silence the guard before the latter raised an alarm. The weather gods were helping. It was raining outside with distant reveberating peals of thunder. In this weather the sentries outside would be in their shelters. The guard's automatic rifle was propped up against the table. Fortunately, the man was fast asleep.

Prashant was looking for a blunt weapon. The empty beer bottle seemed to be his best bet. He glided across the room behind the sleeping guard. Reaching across, he grabbed the bottle just as the man's eyes flickered open. Reflexively, he was reaching for his gun. With all his considerable strength Prashant brought the beer bottle crashing down on the top of the guard's head. The rifle clattered to the ground. The man grunted as he slumped down to the floor unconscious.

The boys were awake and alert. With their blindfolds on, they could not see what was happening. Running to his friends he removed their blindfold and peeled the plaster tapes off their mouths. Working fast, he untied them one by one. They were amazed to see him. Beaten and scared, they could barely believe that Prashant had seized the initiative. Prashant helped them up to their feet. He gestured that they stay silent and away from the cracked window panes.

They turned to the guard and tied him up neatly. They strapped his mouth shut with adhesive tape. Prashant told them in brief about all that had happened. Salim and the others had more information to add. After drinking his beer, their guard had bragged about the group's work. They had a full-fledged research laboratory in Europe. The organization. which had its tentacles all over the world had got together a group of eminent scientists and micro biologists who had developed a new strain of influenza virus. This deadly bug was then sealed in pressurized canisters and locked in small boxes. On a day, which would be decided soon, the virus would be released at international airports and railway stations at major metropolitan cities and at military stations. By using the departure zones of international airports, the would ensure that every continent would have a number of infected people. They estimated that at least half the earth's population, especially the city dwellers would be wiped out in the epidemic that would follow. A few chosen countries would seal their bodies on some premise and keep out the virus from entering. After the death and carnage were over, a new world order would emerge. A limited and highly restricted batch of vaccines and antivirals had been provided to these countries. Eminent men from various field of life, who were sympathetic to the cause would have access to these protective vaccines. They would survive and would chart the course of a new civilization. The box that Saliba had discovered was part of this consignment. The viral consignment was ready and a few final tests were being done in a special lab in the basement. Prashant nodded, he had seen the lab. The man had looked sympathetic. The virus had not been tested fully in humans and the captured boys had been chosen as potential guinea pigs.

12# Saliba's Adventure:

Prashant and the others planned their escape. They would escape from the house and head off separately. If they were together, it would be easier for the guards to track, trace, capture and eliminate them. They estimated that the nearest settlement or town would be a day's walk away. They hoped that at least one or two would reach the nearest town. The authorities would need to be warned. An army or commando unit geared to combat chemical and nuclear warfare would need to be mobilized. There was no time to lose.

Saliba had not heeded Prashant's instructions to wait quietly and patiently. She explored the generator room. The machinery was modern and fully automated. The control panel was sealed. There were two gas towers with a docking port. A road, now closed with sliding doors would allow refueling trucks to drive up and engage.

Saliba guessed that the generator unit needed no human hands for demand driven operations. The maintenance ledge and relaxation room where they had rested was probably meant for the drivers of the gas trucks. The sliding door was also automated and would open on the arrival of designated refueling vehicles.

Saliba realized that there was little else she would learn from the underground generator room. All the secrets lay in the basement laboratory. She followed the route Prashanth had taken earlier. Silently and with care she went up the wooden stairs. Moving over to the barrel stack she examined the casks there. The white paint with red biohazard labels were unnerving. On sensing her presence, a rat scurried to seek shelter somewhere behind the casks. This was reassuring.

More confidently she inspected the barrels. They had the distinctive odor of old wood. The casks felt cool. Each cask had its own cooling system. She kept an open palm on the wooden cask. She could sense the flow of cool fluid through some kind of a capillary system. Suddenly she froze, the doors of the lab were sliding open. There was no time to hide behind the stack of casks. She tried to merge into shadows next to the sliding doors. Scarcely breathing she stayed immobile by the side of the door. The man emerged driving the golf cart with its robotic arms. He did not notice her as he drove past to the barrel stack. The robotic arms engaged the next barrel. After the cask was secured, the cart would turn around. She would be in the man's line of sight. There was no place to hide.

It was an irrational thing to do. But Saliba had no options. The cask had been secured to the golf cart. The electric engine hummed as it turned around. If she stayed there, she would be seen. Saliba slipped in through the open doors into the laboratory complex. She found herself in a large dimly lit room. Fortunately for her there was no one else around. Saliba looked around. There was no equipment here. The working spaces were possibly in closed rooms ahead. The hum of the electric motor was close now. The cart was returning. Saliba moved to a side making herself as inconspicuous as possible in the corner. The cart hummed past. The doors slid shut and clicked closed. Saliba was trapped inside by the closing doors. Stealthily, she moved to a side of the lounge and looked around.

Saliba surveyed the room. She was in a large room with metallic walls. There were a few sofas strewn around and a couple of bean bags. In one corner was a gymnasium of sorts with weights, a punch bag and a high end exercise bicycle. A corridor led out of the room with airlock sealed doors on either side. At the far end of the corridor was a sheer wall. A swiveling surveillance camera scanned the corridor. Saliba tried to merge into the wall as the camera swung in her direction. If she minimized her movements, she might escape the camera security operator's attention.

She could hear the soft hum of an air conditioner. At the far end of the corridor a group of men exited one of the cubicles. They were in an animated discussion. They looked European and at least one of them had a French accent. Two of the men moved on to another room, opening the airlock manually after doing an iris scan. The others went back into the room from where they had emerged. Saliba gave a sigh of relief. If they had decided on a coffee or gym break, she would have been caught.

Saliba walked tiptoed down the corridor. There were airlocked doors on either side. She kept close to the wall, but walked confidently. The security camera was possibly screened by AI and a confident walk could fool it. She was desperately looking for a Safe place to hide while she collected her thoughts and evolved a strategy. She was in luck. There was a small office to her right with a door that was slightly open.

Saliba opened the door a bit more and peeked around. She could see a desk and an empty chair. There was a cupboard in the corner behind or in which she could hide if someone came in. On the wall was a monitoring screen. There were multiple images on the screen. Each room of the laboratory complex was being monitored from here. The corridor was also screened. She could see herself on screen, at the door peeping in. "This must be the room of the laboratory director", thought Saliba. Fortunately, he was not in his chair. If he had been, she would have been discovered.

Thanking her stars for discovering an empty office, she opened the door fully and moved in. her eyes were still on the screen. The multiple images on screen had been replaced by one. Saliba in her dungaree, on the corridor was on screen in a still image. As she watched in fascination, her CV was flashing in top right hand corner of the screen. 'Saliba George, Final year student, English Literature, Government Arts College, Kochi'. A chill crept down her spine.

Someone was using advanced AI and Face Recognition technology. She was absolutely out of her depth here. She felt his presence even before he touched her. A powerful hand clamped over her mouth and another around a waist. Saliba struggled fruitlessly for a minute and then gave in. The grip she was in was intoxicating and overpowering.

13# Saliba's awakening:

The man who held her was very strong and tall. She could feel the rippling hardness of her muscular frame through her dungarees. His voice was soothing and resonant. He spoke with a British accent. "I am Richard, a cell biologist". Saliba frowned. The name was familiar. She remembered reading an article of Gene editing using biological scissors. I am in charge of this laboratory. I saw you coming into the laboratory and I was hoping that you would drop in". Saliba had stopped struggling now. Holding her firm against his warm torso, the man slid a large warm hand over her body, lingering over her soft curves and firm abdomen as he checked her for weapons. Finding none, his arm around her waist relaxed. She remained dazed, leaning against him. She could hear and feel the throb of his bounding heart.

He smiled as he eased her into a chair. He

sat in his sofa, across the table, facing her. It took him a minute to get his emotions and thoughts in order. His voice was controlled and his narration professional again. "Well, my Indian beauty, you have guts, following your friends after they were captured. Tell me. Who else in there with you?". Saliba guessed that the man would not know about Prashant. "I came alone" – she said. The man looked at her quizzically for a moment. He then nodded his head as though he had just taken an important decision. Saliba was trying to read his mind. But Richard's barriers were up. Saliba could not decipher his thoughts. He seemed pensive and lost in a world of his own.

Saliba kept looking at Richard. He seemed strangely familiar. She felt a profound intuitive longing in his presence. Yet she was also aware that that he was the enemy. He was likely to kill her and her friends. He was also probably hatching some horrendous scheme of mass murder. She could barely contain or express the intense arousal she experienced at his touch.

He was a handsome man – Thought Saliba. He was probably British, judging from his crisp accent. Well above six foot in height – he was an impressive figure. Yet, the way he moved and spoke and his delicate eloquent hands with overgrown knobby fingers gave him a professorial air. He walked over to a refrigerator and opened the door. The wooden box he extracted from it was similar to the one Saliba had found on the forest floor. He brought the box close to his face. It took Saliba a while to realize that he was using his iris to scan and to biometrically open the lock. There was a metallic click as the box snapped open. A crystal glass vial was extracted and the box snapped shut.

There was a rack of syringes next to the refrigerator. Saliba watched as Richard expertly snapped open a syringe and loaded it. Saliba sprang up to escape and then sat down as he looked at her. "Don't worry. If I wanted to kill you, you would be dead by now. I am giving you this vaccine because I want you to live and be yourself. I want you, to bear my children in the new world." He strode over to Saliba. Standing behind her, his fingers snapped open the front buttons of her dungaree. He pulled the Dungaree off her shoulders. Dabbing her arm with an antiseptic wipe, he waited a few seconds before plunging the needle into her deltoid. Saliba relished the dull pain as he rested her cheek against his forearm. Richard ruffled her hair before buttoning her dungaree closed again. He was getting a hold over himself again. His hands were soft and his manner professional. "It will be few days before you develop immunity". There were lab coats hanging from a rack on the wall. He wore one and tossed over another coat to her. "Wear this, he said- I will show you around the lab and tell you a story".

Richard helped Saliba to her feet. She was giddy and leaned against him. The intense sensual attraction she felt for him was now tempered with the realization that she had to stop him from mass murder even if she were to die trying. They walked out to the corridor. Richard opened one of the labs. There was a barrel with its Biohazard seal on it. Saliba recoiled in horror as Richard unscrewed a plastic lid on the cask and dipped his finger in what appeared to be a clear fluid. A brought a drop of the fluid to his tongue. "Tasteless but potent". He turned to Saliba. "Tell me what you know about nanoparticles in drug delivery".

Saliba had read about nanoparticles which could be used for targeted drug delivery. Richard continued his tirade. "Nano particle encapsulated drugs can be guided to selected targets. The barrels you saw outside contain nanoparticle suspensions. These particles encapsulate a retroviral gene crafted using CRISPR-Cas gene editing technology".

"We identified a specific protein which binds with the subgroup of endothelin found at the Blood Brain Barrier. By embedding an antibody to this protein into the nano-capsule, we can make sure that our gene charged nanoparticles home on to the Brain. When the nanoparticle fuses with endothelin, the Blood Barrier opens allowing the particles entry into the otherwise pristine Brain circulation. These particles remain lodged in brain capillaries until we activate them".

Saliba's head was reeling. "How will you activate the particles?". "We have formulated a specific code which will release a small electromagnetic pulse from your cell phones. On receiving this pulse, the nano particle will release the doctored gene into brain matter. This gene particle is like a virus. Just as a virus hijacks a cell's mechanism to make its own protein, we can use the nanoparticle receiver to deliver a concept, a thought or a belief to each captivated brain".

It all sounded extremely dystopic to Saliba. Nanoparticles being used to convey modified retroviral particles to the brain. Activating these nano particles through viral codes embedded in cell phones. There were other unanswered questions. How would the vaccine help against this nano particle-based attack on humanity. And why were the barrels labelled as biohazards.

Richard smiled. I will answer the second question first. "The biohazard label prevents unwelcome intrusions and investigations. Our mercenary guards are also kept in leash with the promise and threat of unfathomable violence and death". "The vaccine", Richard continued, "protects you from a nano attack", Richard continued. "The antibodies triggered by the vaccine deactivates endothelin receptors. Nano particles targeting endothelin receptors will no longer get access to the brain. The modified retrovirus can no longer take over the neurons. It is the genetically modified brain which will be susceptible to mind control. Nano tagged brains will behave in a particular manner to coded inputs. These inputs may be through Television, newspapers or through your mobile phones. To understand Brain Control we have to understand how the brain works".

They were back in Richard's office. Richard guided her to a mini sofa. They settled down in the sofa. Richard's arm was round her shoulders. She felt wonderfully awake and wanted. Richard continued. "The brain is our organ of intelligence. Intelligence is the ability to acquire, process and to act upon information. All living creatures have intelligence. Plants grow their roots towards water and present their photosynthetic foliage to sunlight. Single celled amoebae move towards nutrition and away from toxins. Our sensory organs provide information input. Our speech organs and motor systems execute the response decided by the cognitive or information processing unit. Information processing and decision making involves education, training and our genetic endowment".

"Artificial intelligence paradigms have the same three phases. Information is garnered or fed in, data archives are sieved for correct results and the operative arm executes a task or frames an answer. Exclusivity and individuality of human decision-making rests upon our genetic code. Wisdom, judgement, value systems and character traits reside here. This is the target of our nano tagged spliced genes. They will take away man's free will. We will decide how humanity should behave, think and act".

Saliba clutched his powerful arms as he kissed her. He paused, holding her close. "Those of us who have received this vaccine will retain our free will. The child you will bear for me will also be a free man. Human destiny will be in our hands". Richard was unbuttoning her coat as she spoke. The office door lock clicked as he pressed a remote button.

Afterward they held each other close for a long long time. Richard helped Saliba to her feet. There was a long silence. "My time is over. I have done my bit to reshape the world. My legacy will change the course of civilization. Our son will continue my work. We will work in varied and often conflicting spheres, but towards the same universal truths. We both have unfinished work and promises to keep. Saliba's eyes brimmed over. Richard was saying goodbye. She could not fathom why?

14# The Boys Escape:

After trussing up the guard, Prashant and the three boys made for the front door. Carefully they opened the door. It was raining outside. This was reassuring. The sentries would be cowered down beneath rain capes and visibility was poor. Shutting the door softly behind them, they crouched behind bushes in the porch. Prashant pointed out the sentry posts. He warned them of the moat and suggested possible routes for escape into the forest without getting caught. The stakes were high. If they got caught again, the guards would make sure they would not run again.

The rain was coming down in sheets. Rashid, Salim and Rishab sprinted across the yard. They climbed down into the moat and then clambering up the opposite walls merged into the forest. The sentries did not spot them. There were no shots or shouts.

Prashant heaved a sigh of relief. He was sure the boys would make it to civilization through the forest. Once they contacted the police, a search party or an anti-naxal commando unit would be mobilized.

He decided to get Saliba. Together, they too would head out for the highway. Opening the front door, he eased himself in. He shut the door softly behind him. Carefully he climbed down to the laboratory complex. The barrels were still there. The lab doors were closed. The trap door was open. He climbed down into the generator room. Where was Saliba. The maintenance ledge was empty. There was no sign of her.

He checked the generator room again. The ramp door was closed. Climbing back to the laboratory he checked behind the barrels finding only a quizzical looking rat. Saliba had disappeared. He peeped into the laboratory through the glass pane. He could see a man and a woman walking around in their laboratory suits. There was no sign of

Saliba. If she was not in the building, she would have escaped through the front door.

"Saliba must have got out" thought Prashant. He wondered where she was. If she were hiding in the forest, she would have seen the boys escape and gone with them. Knowing Saliba, Prashant doubted if she would leave him and run. There was another possibility. She may have tried to track Reena while he was rescuing the boys. To track Reena she would just have to follow the jeep tracks. – he guessed. If she were trying to track Reena, she would be in danger. Prashant decided to follow the jeep tracks himself. He got out of the house, skirting the observation posts. He made his way through the dense undergrowth to where he expected the jeep track to be. In a short while he found it. Walking was easier now. The thought of Saliba walking alone in the dark was disconcerting. He hurried to catch up. At a slow jog, he set off in the dark. He would catch up with Saliba and together – they would rescue Reena.

15# All Hell Breaks Loose:

There was a knock at the door. Richard walked across from the sofa and opened the door. At the door was a security sentry of the laboratory. He looked perturbed. The sentry guarding the prisoners had not called in to report. They tried to get him on his handset. There was no response. Richard strode across to the monitoring screen and flicked a button.   The lawns around the bungalow appeared on the screen. They could see the sentry posts. The rain had ebbed a bit and visibility was good. The sentries were relaxed and alert. All was well there. Ricard flicked another switch. The bungalow rooms appeared on screen. The conference room was empty.

The room where the boys had been kept now lit up. The boys were missing. The scotch tape and ropes used to bind and gag them lay scattered on the floor. There was an exclamation from Richard. The sentry, all trussed up and gagged was coming awake. Richard turned to the security man. "Call back all our men. I will be giving fresh orders soon. Call in the boats for distributing the consignment.

The security man left, barking orders into his communication set. Holding Saliba by the arm, Richard closed the door. He walked her back to the sofa and plonked her down. He was scrolling through images on the screen. She could see Prashant on screen, beaning the guard with a beer bottle. Richard was zooming in of Prasanth's face after pausing the video. Facial identification software took just a few seconds before labelling him. 'Prasanth Singh- alumnus of IIT Mumbai'. Richard was scanning the generator room video now. Saliba and Richard could be seen, helping each other with their dungarees. Richard switched off the screen.

Saliba was looking at him. Richard did not look angry. A deep resignation was registered and reflected in his face and demeanor. "I am glad you came. My time was due. My work is complete. I will live again through our child. Take care of him". He paused for a few seconds. Prasanth looks a decent youth. Make a future with him. Remember what I told you. We have been using Nano tagged gene slicing for more than a year. I have trained the personnel in two major labs in Europe on bulk production of these brain control particles. These barrels that you saw hold nanoparticle concentrates. They are prepared for use as aerosols. Once they are released into a ventilation system, everyone in the room will be infected. The vaccine is given only to those we identify as future leaders. You will be one of the select few, left with free will. You and our son"- he patted her belly affectionately. Richard was leaving. Saliba sank back into the sofa sobbing as Richard left the room.

 hurried back into his office. He clicked a button and a set of TV screens came alive. Saliba could see the trussed up sentry on the floor and the empty room. She could hear his voice in the corridor giving orders to his men. One of the guards walked in. Saliba's arms were twisted behind and she was tied to the chair. Richard was speaking on a radio now. His voice was clear and strong, yet deferential. "The prisoners have escaped". He seemed to listen to some orders from the other end.

Turning to his men, he gave them the order. "Call back all the men and load the barrels on to the waiting boats. Operation universal joy is being launched. There was a flurry of activity. One of the men was on the radio now – calling back their army from the forest. Richard had connected to the internet. Saliba saw him type on the screen – "Activate Universal Joy"- Agents of joy to be released at 2300 tomorrow.

All over the world agents were receiving the alert. A few private airplanes were being readied at Kochi Airport. They had the logo of a private courier on their wings. A small fleet of courier trunks set out on the highway to a rendezvous point near Wayanad. At air ports and railway stations all over the country sympathetic officials were donning their uniforms. They had received their instructions. Their job would be to ensure that the release of the canisters into the air circulation system would occur as rehearsed. Prof Amin contacted his travel agent. His conference dates in the middle east had been advanced by two days. The necessary changes in his travel portfolio were implemented. Prominent scholars from many part of the world similarly changed their air tickets. After Nanoparticles were disseminated, they would start a disinformation campaign. They would initially target world opinion and later ferment dissent and rebellions. The nanoparticles in the brain would appear to be small foci of calcification in case any of the victims underwent MR evaluation of the brain.

16# Blasts in the Bungalow:

Reena woke up. Abdullah was sitting on a chair- watching her. He had a loaded syringe in his hand. "Your friends have escaped. We are starting the operation now. I will give you this injection to protect you. Reena sat up. She smiled as he plunged the needle into her arm. She loved him and trusted him implicitly. It took her a while to get ready. Together, they went down to the jeep. The guards were ready – weapons slung over their shoulders. There was an air of eager anticipation. Abdullah led his men in a short prayer. The preparatory phase was over. The action was starting. They started the jeep and headed for the bungalow.

Prashant was walking and intermittently jogging along the mud track looking for Saliba. The forest was dense here and seething with assorted forms of life. He focused on the path. He should not trip over a python or bump into an elephant. He was tired now. But the forest was no place to snooze. Where was Saliba. Had she been taken by some predator?

He was walking now. Suddenly he heard the roar of an approaching vehicle. The road was curving ahead. A distant glow of headlights could be seen through the foliage. They would be heading back to the bungalow. Prashant stumbled as he tried to move into the forest. After a moment of consternation, he realized that he had stumbled on a fallen tree trunk. A surge of anger coursed through him. The jeep was drawing nearer. In a few minutes it would navigate the curve and illuminate the road with its head beams.

The jeep occupants would not see him unless he stood on the road as they drove round the bend. Prashant pulled the dried log across the road. He added a few rocks for additional effect. Scooping up a pile of soggy leaves he covered the obstacles. The log and rock were camouflaged effectively. He hoped to fool the driver into thinking that the tree leaves were innocuous. If the jeep were coming up fast, the driver would lose control.

He hoped that the jeep would come around the curve fast and crash into the forest after hitting the logs. He moved into the bushes as the roar of the jeep grew nearer. The headlights could be seen now. The jeep was coming fast. Turning the corner, the driver spotted the leaves and tried to slow down. If he had seen the log and rocks, he could probably have screeched to a halt. The leaves made the barricade look soft and negotiable. The jeep jumped as one the front wheels hit a rock. It then bounced down on the log. The crash was followed by the jeep overturning. The lights of the jeep were still on. The wheels were spinning and the engine still running. The driver had lost consciousness. The tall man, the group leader seemed unhurt. Prashant watched as he helped Reena – who seemed dazed, but uninjured out of the over turned jeep. He turned off the jeep's engine and lights.

One of the guards had broken a leg. The leader and his unhurt body guards moved the two injured men to one side. They were obviously well versed in first Aid. The men righted the jeep. The tall man was splinting his soldier's leg with a proficiency that suggested expert surgical skills. After checking for petrol leaks and structural damage, the men started the jeep engine again. Prashant watched as the guards turned the jeep around. They checked the log and rocks with the cover of leaves. The men looked at one another. They looked around the forest around. One of the guards pointed his gun into the bushes. The tall man raised his hand to stop him. They put the injured men in the back seat of the jeep. The tree trunk and the rocks were moved off the road. The tall man gave instructions. The soldiers would be taken for treatment to a private hospital. They were to say that their jeep had overturned when they encountered a wild elephant on the highway.

The guards set off with the jeep, back down the mud track. The tall man and Reena walked straight ahead. He was speaking into his handset. All his attention was on the road ahead. Prashant looked around. The jeep lights had faded into the forest and the growl of the jeeps engine was a barely perceptible hum in the distance. He could heat the tall mans voice receding down the road as he walked briskly with Reena by his side. He found a crowbar by the roadside. It had fallen out of the jeep when it overturned. This would do as a weapon. With the crowbar over his Right shoulder, he followed Reena and the tall man. When he got a chance, he would smash the tall man's head and rescue Reena.

17# Winding up:

Saliba could hear voices and sounds above. The guards on patrol were trooping back into the bungalow. Through the open door she could see guards hurrying around with golf carts and trolleys. The casks were being shifted down the ramp for loading on boats. The back door of the laboratory was open. She heard the chug of boats out on the lake. She guessed the boxes would be taken to some pick up point by boat. Waiting trucks would carry them to the airport and the courier planes in their private hanger. Richard was in the lab - supervising the final steps of loading. He would now move on to the jetty to confirm that all was in order. He paused and looked into his office. Saliba was on the chair. Her hands were still tied behind. He strode across and kissed her one last time on the lips. Reaching behind her, he undid the knot that fastened her hands. He turned and strode away towards the ramp. Saliba saw him wiping a tear off his cheek.

He was sacrificing something that meant a lot to him.

Saliba turned to free her hands. The knot was now open and the bind was not too tight. No one was watching her. She freed one hand and then the other. Two men were wheeling out a trolley from the lab. There was empty cart parked close to the wall. She strode over and sat on the driver's seat. The key was in the ignition slot. She maneuvered the cart around and headed for the laboratory door. Fortunately for her door was opening as another cart moved in with its cargo. The man driving the cart had seen her with Richard. She hoped that the men were not aware that her disloyalty had been exposed. She gave him a small wave and he waved back. The cart was now outside the laboratory door. Richard was nowhere in sight as Saliba escaped the lab.

There was a man loading a barrel on to his golf cart. Saliba waited behind till the man turned towards the lab. Saliba pretended to inspect and to arrange the barrels in order. The man's golf cart was inside the laboratory complex. As soon as the sliding laboratory door closed, she ran for the stairs- but stopped suddenly. The front door was open and someone was entering. She quickly lifted the trap door and hurried down into the generator room. Fortunately, the generator room was still empty. She hid herself behind some gasoline tanks and waited.

She sat with her head in her hands as she tried to collect her thoughts. She had surrendered her body and her soul to Richard. She believed all that he said he had done and what he was doing. But was it morally or ethically correct. Was it right to take away man's free will. The right of each man to plot his own destiny was God given. Could this be usurped by an intellectual elite.

If the nanoparticles with their crisper cas modified genes were to transfect most of humanity, humans would be like honey bees.

They would be diligent team workers in the service of a chosen few with free will. She believed that democracy with all its insanity was superior to aa autocracy with an unelected monarch. Why was Richard doing this if he were planning to die. There was a lot she did not know. She remembered Richard's words. We all had to do what we think is right and then leave outcomes to fate or God.

In a few hours nanoparticle aerosols would start transfecting people. This mass of humanity would be blissfully oblivious to the fact that their ability to reason had been compromised. Who would call the shots in this scenario. Would the fourth estate rule or decide who would rule nations. Had Richard suffered remorse over the consequences of his work. The laboratory would be churning out barrels of nano particles even if Richard opted out.

She realized that the consequences of unfettered nanoparticle production could be disastrous. Natural corrections to excesses would be compromised. This had to contained. If this outrage was to be prevented some one had to act now. With a sickening sensation , she realized that the only person who could save the conscience of humanity was she herself.

Khalil was still giving orders on his radiophone – as he and Reena walked swiftly down the path. They were near the bungalow now. Prashant had been following them. If they reached the building, Khalil would be ensconced in a protective cordon of security guards again. If he had a chance to rescue Reena, it was now.

Prashant ran up behind them, taking care to synchronize his footfalls with Khalil's. The tall giant was immersed in conversation on his radiophone. Prashant would have nailed him in a moment. Reena spied him as he closed in. Shouting "No" – she pushed Abdullah away to safety as Prashant's crowbar came crashing down. The bar grazed

Khalil's shoulder.   He was unhurt. Khalil realized that Reena had saved his life. He also realized that the assailant was known to her and was potentially trying to rescue her.

Prashant looked amazed at Reena's change in loyalty.   In a millisecond, Khalil had recovered his balance. Whirling around in one fluid movement, he knocked Prashant unconscious with the butt of his rifle. Stepping over his unconscious body, Khalil raised his gun to fire. Reena was pushing his gun away. She fell to her knees and begged him to spare Prashant's life.

 Khalil looked at her one moment. He took a moment to sling his gun back over his shoulder. He knelt down and felt Prashant's pulse. He looked at Reena. "Your friend will survive, he said". Holding her by the arm he hurried on toward the forest bungalow. All the lights in the bungalow seemed to be on. There were guards waiting for them at the door. Seeing their leader, they snapped to attention as he walked in through the front door. The security chief was giving him a completion report. The barrels had been neatly stocked on the waiting boats in the lake. Richard was down by the lakeside giving final instructions to the boatmen. Khalil got up. He went to the front door. He would walk down to the boathouse to meet Richard. He wanted to discuss with him his plans to opt out. Reena went with him.

18# Saliba sets the House on Fire:

Saliba had heard the leader return. A crazy plan had been concocted in her mind. She checked the gasolene tanks. The tanks were nearly full. She looked around and found a crow bar. With all she might, she hammered a hole in one of the tanks. Gasoline started gurgling out.   The smell was over powering. She ran up the wooden ladder. Lifting the trap door, she got out.

A guard had heard the hammering and was coming to investigate. A cigarette dangled from the corner of his mouth. Saliba hid behind the trap door as the guard stepped on to the wooden ladder. Looking around, he climbed down. As Saliba watched in horror, the man paused to flick his half-burned cigarette down. Saliba sprinted up the steps and out through the front door as a tongue of flame shot up from the generator room. Behind her the earth rumbled as the tanks of gasoline exploded. Flying debris whizzed past her head as she sprinted towards the forest. The blast of the underground explosion lifted her off the ground, hurling her into the branches of a tree. She lost consciousness for a few minutes. Slowly she come to feeling the intense heat of the burning inferno behind her.

The bungalow had disappeared to give way to a fiery crater. She ran through the forest along a track she chanced upon. The fire lit up the forest like a giant lamp. Saliba kept running. She must have been a mile away when she saw a body lying sprawled across the path. She went closer. She realized that it was Prashant. For a moment she thought that Prashant was dead. Choking back a sob, she knelt beside him. She almost laughed aloud in relief. Prashant was alive and he was coming to. Groggily he looked at Saliba and then he sat up. They looked behind them. The flames were dying down, doused by a fresh spell of monsoon rain.

Saliba and Prashant walked down the path.

As they walked, Saliba recounted all that Richard told her. Barrels of spliced gene tagged nanoparticles had been loaded on boats sailing towards the harbor. These would be used to create aerosols in work places and travel nodes. Over a period of time, when a fair proportion of humanity were transfected, mobile phones, newspapers and broadcasts would activate nano chips in peoples brains making them submissive and susceptible to brain washing and opinion creation.

Saliba had destroyed the lab. But Richard said there were other labs too. Saliba and Prashant continued walking. Ahead, they could see a tree house in the clearing. Behind the house was a rock face and water fall. Beyond the tree house the path ran around the mountain. Saliba and Prashant ran along the path, stopping occasionally to catch their breath. The fire in the forest had died down behind them. Day was dawning. Scintillating rays of the rising sun sent probing fingers over the horizon.

19# The Elephant and the Lion:

The two of them hurried along down the soggy track. By midafternoon, they had reached a larger road. Saliba expected the highway to be south coast. They headed in that direction. They were exhausted now, hungry and thirsty. Saliba kept looking over her shoulder hoping for a vehicle which could give them a lift. They were out of the dense forest now. There was a glassy pain ahead. A green hill loomed before them. On the other side of the hill would be the highway. Saliba was tired. Prashant volunteered to climb the grassy slope to scout out the best route to the road. She sat under a tree while Prashant jogged ahead. She nodded off to sleep.

Saliba woke up hearing Prashant shout. He was running down the road. Behind him and catching up rapidly was a large Tusker. Saliba screamed. This was Chackakomban, the lone tusker who had maimed and killed a large number of people before merging into the anonymity of the dense forest again. Run into the Prashant was screaming. Saliba turned and ran. She reached the tree line and jumped behind the trunk of a giant tree. If she stayed immobile behind big trees in the forest Chackakomban would not bother to chase her. She heard Prashant scream. Peeking from behind the tree she saw a horrendous scene. Chackakomban had picked up Prashant in his trunk. He threw him into the air. Prashant landed on the path. The elephant was moving toward Prashant as he lay on the road clutching his leg. Saliba screamed and tried to distract the majestic Tusker. She threw stones at him screaming for Prasanth to move away from the pachyderm's path. Prashant's leg was broken. He could not get up. He looked at Saliba and then at the elephant moving in for the kill.

The tusker came to an abrupt halt just a few feet away from the fallen Prashant. Saliba heard the roar of a motorcycle. A powerful motor bike drew up next to Prashant. The rider took off his helmet. Saliba gasped. It was Richard. Chackakomban looked bemused as Richard parked his bike. Richard licked up a stck which Saliba had thrown on the road to distract the elephant. He now removed Prashant's Jean belt. With the stick and the belt Richard fashioned a splint for Prashant's leg. Cradling Prashant in his arms he carried him to where Saliba was hiding, behind the tree.

There was grunt a from Chackakomban. This large white man had ignored him completely and snatched away his victim. The bottled up anger and frustration against the human race would not allow him to spare Prashant. He turned towards the tree. The forest was his. He would pluck out the maimed human and finish off the job.

Richard stepped out in front of the aggrieved elephant. He smacked the tusker hard on his swinging trunk. Chackakomban took a step back. They were both on the road now- man and elephant faced each other in a test of dignity, will and strength. It was drizzling. A peal of thunder in the distance startled the elephant. He walked back a few steps, never taking his eyes off this diminutive human who was challenging him. Lightning flashed again and the roar of thunder was deafening. Chackakomban lost his composure. He charged Richard and knocked him down. Kneeling, he impaled him with his magnificent tusks.

The elephant rose to his feet, with the man impaled on his tusks. Richard was dead. Chackakomban stood straight with his trunk raised and his Gory price dripping blood down his tusks. Saliba and Prasanth watched, frozen in petrified despair. Would the tusker turn upon them. Saliba swore to herself that she would not abandon Prashant. She would die with him. Then Chackakomban did something amazing. Kneeling down he pulled Ricards body off his Tusls with his trunk. He laid him gently by the side of the road. With his trunk he broke small leafy branches off a peepul tree. He covered Richards body with the Foliage. Stepping back he raised his trunk into the air. His deafening Trumpet muffled the peals of thunder. The rain came down in a torrent of sorrowful cleansing. Chackakomban trumpeted again- long and mournful. He then turned and trotted away. Was it the rain and was it giant teardrops washing blood off the glorious elephant's tusks.

20# Rescue:

Saliba sat with Prashant's head resting on her lap. His leg was fractured and the jagged end of the fractured bone had punctured his skin. Richard's bespoke splint made the pain bearable. His chest was hurting and he had probably punctured a lung with some fractured ribs. He was conscious and in pain. His leg throbbed and he was having difficulty in moving his foot. Saliba loosened the belt on his splint to allow blood to flow through. They would have to wait till some vehicle came down the jungle road.

Richards motor cycle was standing on the other side. Saliba knew how to rid it. Prashant suggested that she leave him and take the bike to town to get help. He was too unstable to sit behind her on a two wheeler. Saliba refused to leave him alone. There would be predators around who would attack an injured man. If she were there with him, they had a better chance. In case no one came that way, when the sun was up she would try to go and get help. Prashant had drifted off to sleep. His consciousness was now waxing and waning. He needed help and he needed it soon.

A little later Saliba heard the chug of an engine. Some sort of a vehicle was coming up the road from the forest. She made a pillow of leaves for Prashant. His eyes were closed but he mumbled something as she went to the road. Saliba waited by the roadside. It was getting dark. It would be tragic if the vehicle went past without stopping. They paused by the roadside. It was an open jeep. Even from a distance Saliba could see that there were two people in it. Saliba walked out to the center of the road to wave the jeep down. With the head beams in her eyes, she could not see the occupants. The jeep slowed and then rumbled to a stop. The lights were dimmed and then doused. Saliba blinked and reared back in alarm. Khalil was in the driver's seat. Seated next to him was Reena. Saliba shuddered. She had just brought his bungalow down and blown up Khalil's operations. Here she was, at his mercy. She would have run into the forest. But Prashant was helpless. If he did not reach a hospital fast he could lose his leg or even his life.

Khalil got off the jeep and walked up to Saliba. Reena followed him. She was smiling. Saliba was strangely reassured. "I heard the Tusker's magnificent trumpet call. I had heard it in Africa once. The Zulus call it the last Trumpet. The call is given by the lead Tusker in a valley to announce the death of a king". Saliba pointed to Richards body covered with leaves and branches by Chakkakomban. Abdulla went and knelt before him. He touched his forehead to the ground in a gesture of respect.

"Abdulla rose to his feet. "Richard was a great man. He was brave, a lion king. He was also a brilliant scientist. He devised the whole nano-molecule carrier. He also designed the gene that would make humanity conform. He felt that a few select souls could guide humanity to eternal greatness without wars and violence. Of late however, he started having some remorse. He wanted to opt out. He was waiting for you to share and perpetuate his genes before he ended his life". Saliba blushed. "Don't worry. No one except the three of us will know your secret. Prashant will take care of you.

There was a groan of pain from behind the tree. Prashant was waking up. Khalil and Reena went with Saliba. He closed his eyes when he saw the man he had tried to kill walk up with his two friends. Kahil did an expert examination. Prashant's pulse was racing. His breathing was shallow. Khali could feel ai bubbles under the skin on his chest. Prashant had multiple rib fractures. One of the fractured ribs had punctured his lung. His Tibia fracture required urgent attention. The pulses in his foot were palpable but feeble. The foot could be saved with early surgery. He would also require a tube in his chest to drain out blood and leaking air. He would require oxygen and a few units of blood. They had to get him to hospital fast.

The three of them carried Prashant to the jeep. He was laid out on the back seat. Khalil strapped him down so that he would not roll off. Reena sat next to him to soothe and reassure him. She would also stabilize him when the jeep ride turned bumpy. They started the jeep. Saliba followed on Richard's bike. They drove slowly. Bumps could be painful to Prashant.

They reached the highway in half an hour. There was a private medical college an hour's drive away. They reported to the casualty. Prasanth was wheeled into intensive care and then to OR. Khalil had telephoned a contact in the forest department. Richard's body was retrieved. TV and Newspapers splashed news snippets of a British hiker who had been gored to death in the forest by a rogue elephant.

Prashanth made a remarkably fast recovery. He was hobbling around on a crutch in three weeks. He married Saliba in a quiet ceremony attended by only close relatives and friends. Prashant was still in a cast. They were in a hurry. Prashant had been selected as a manager in one of Boeings R and D units. The aircraft industry behemoth was undergoing a major revamp and was scouting for exceptional international talent. Prashant had interned with them during and after his IIT Bombay phase before business school. He would initially be in a desk job but would need to travel after his leg healed fully. Saliba could accompany him. She would join as an assistant editor in the New York Times.

Epilogue:

Five years passed. Boeing had revived its flailing fortunes. A new series of commercial aircraft launched by the company were an unequivocal success.
Prashant was the vice president in charge of product development.

An Arab Sheik had recently acquired a middle eastern airline and was in the process of a rapid expansion of his fleet. Prashant was scheduled to meet up with him on a social cum business get together in the company guest house where the Sheik was staying with his wife and young son.

Prashant had taken Saliba with him. She had just returned from a tour of Europe documenting the dynamics of post war reconstruction in Ukraine. Prasanth and Khalil had interacted multiple times on this project. Saliba had no idea who the Arab Sheik was.

The sheik himself opened the door. Saliba and Reena squealed in surprised delight on their surprise reunion after 5 years. Their children were almost the same age.

Reena was working in the sheiks airline and was in charge of operations. Her son Abdul, was a brilliant student who swore that he wanted to be a space explorer.

Khalil turned to Saliba. What about your son. " Oh, he wants to be a Neurosurgeon. He says that the greatest of secrets is not in the far reaches of space but in the Neurons and Synapses of the human brain".
"What is his name?" Khalil was looking at her as he asked the question. "Oh-it is Simba", she said, with a sly wink. "You know- the Lion King".

*****